Gertrude Chandler Warner's

THE BOXCAR CHILDREN

GRAPHIC NOVELS

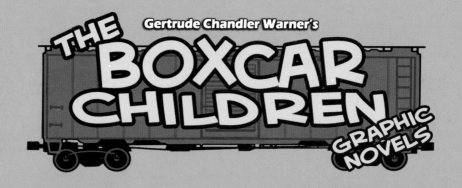

MYSTERY IN THE SAND

The Aldens are spending sunny days at the shore and summer nights in a mobile home right on the beach! One morning, Benny finds a gold necklace in the sand. Soon a search for its owner begins, and a trail of clues leads the children to Tower House. What will the Box[illegible] Children find in the strange old ma[illegible]

THE BOXCAR CHILDREN
GRAPHIC NOVELS

THE BOXCAR CHILDREN
SURPRISE ISLAND
THE YELLOW HOUSE MYSTERY
MYSTERY RANCH
MIKE'S MYSTERY
BLUE BAY MYSTERY
SNOWBOUND MYSTERY
TREE HOUSE MYSTERY
THE HAUNTED CABIN MYSTERY
THE AMUSEMENT PARK MYSTERY
THE PIZZA MYSTERY
THE CASTLE MYSTERY
THE WOODSHED MYSTERY
THE LIGHTHOUSE MYSTERY
MOUNTAIN TOP MYSTERY
HOUSEBOAT MYSTERY
BICYCLE MYSTERY
MYSTERY IN THE SAND

Gertrude Chandler Warner's

THE BOXCAR CHILDREN
MYSTERY IN THE SAND

Adapted by Joeming Dunn
Illustrated by Ben Dunn

Henry Alden

Watch

Jessie Alden

Violet Alden

Benny Alden

Visit us at www.albertwhitman.com.

Adapted by Joeming Dunn
Illustrated by Ben Dunn
Colored by Robby Bevard
Lettered by Joeming Dunn & Doug Dlin
Edited by Stephanie Hedlund
Interior layout and design by Kristen Fitzner Denton
Cover art by Ben Dunn

Library of Congress Cataloging-in-Publication Data
is available from the Library of Congress.

10 9 8 7 6 5 4 3 2 1 LB 15 14 13 12 11

MYSTERY IN THE SAND

Contents

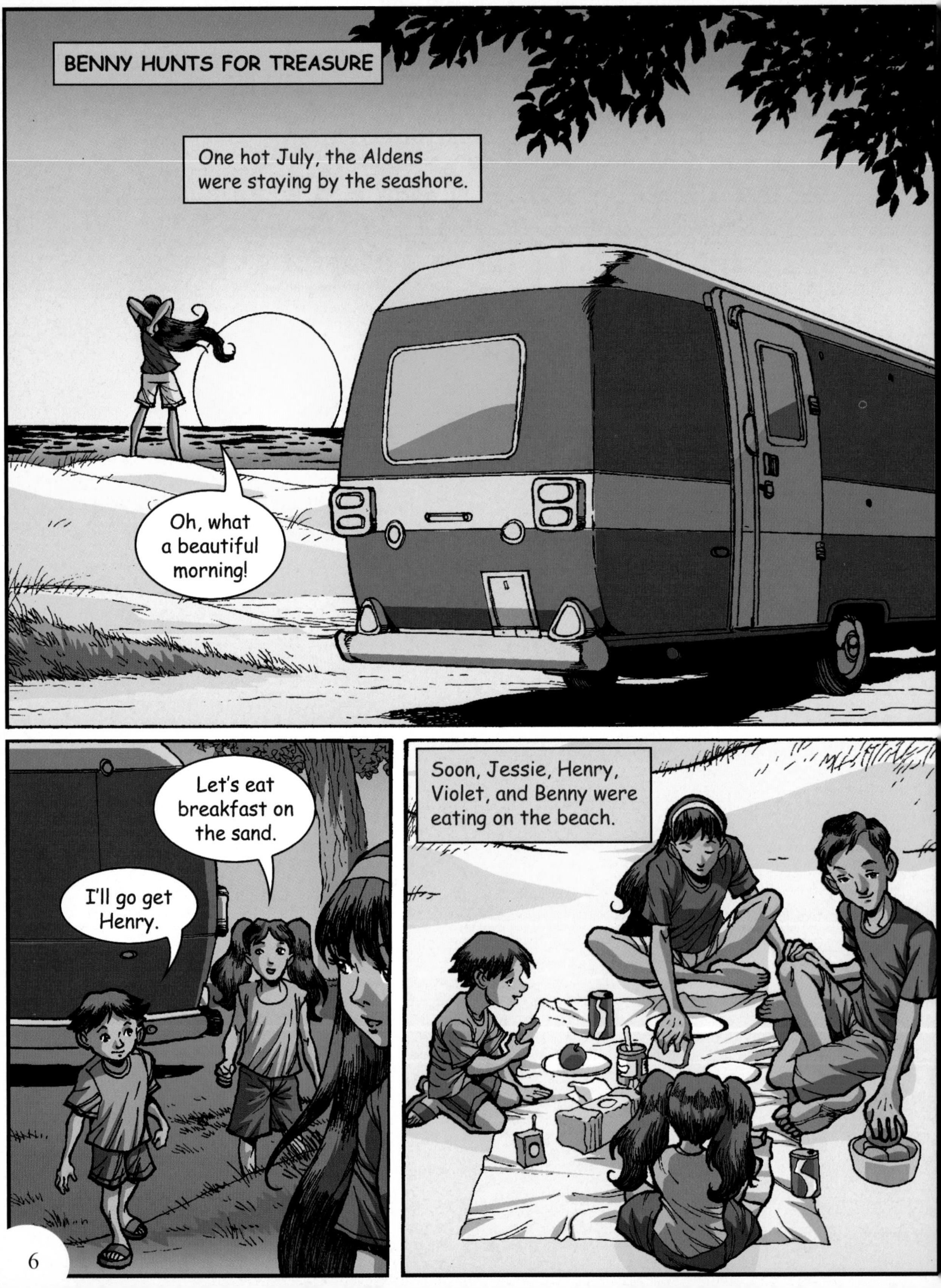
BENNY HUNTS FOR TREASURE
One hot July, the Aldens were staying by the seashore.
Oh, what a beautiful morning!
Let's eat breakfast on the sand.
I'll go get Henry.
Soon, Jessie, Henry, Violet, and Benny were eating on the beach.

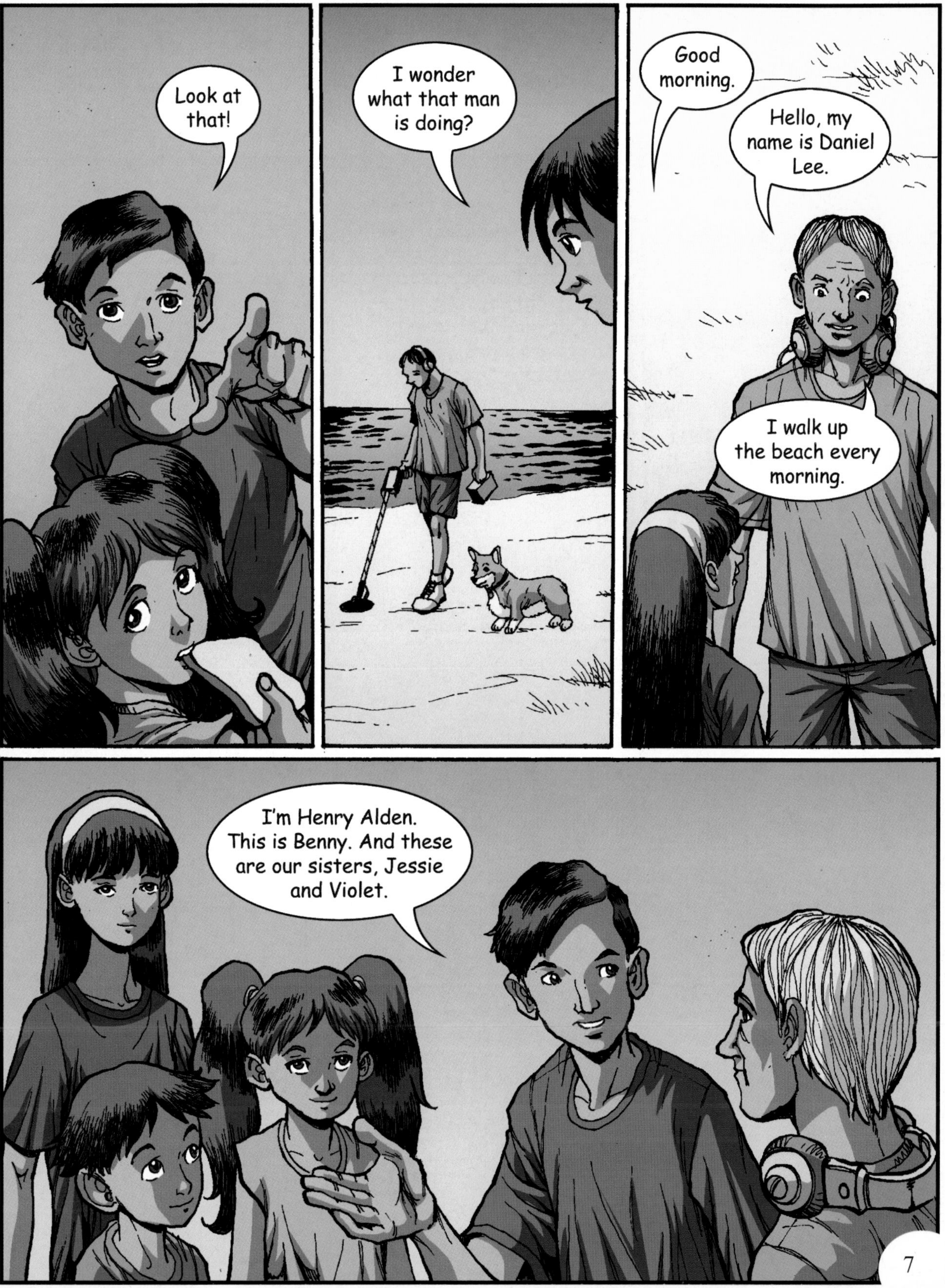
Look at that!
I wonder what that man is doing?
Good morning.
Hello, my name is Daniel Lee.
I walk up the beach every morning.
I'm Henry Alden. This is Benny. And these are our sisters, Jessie and Violet.

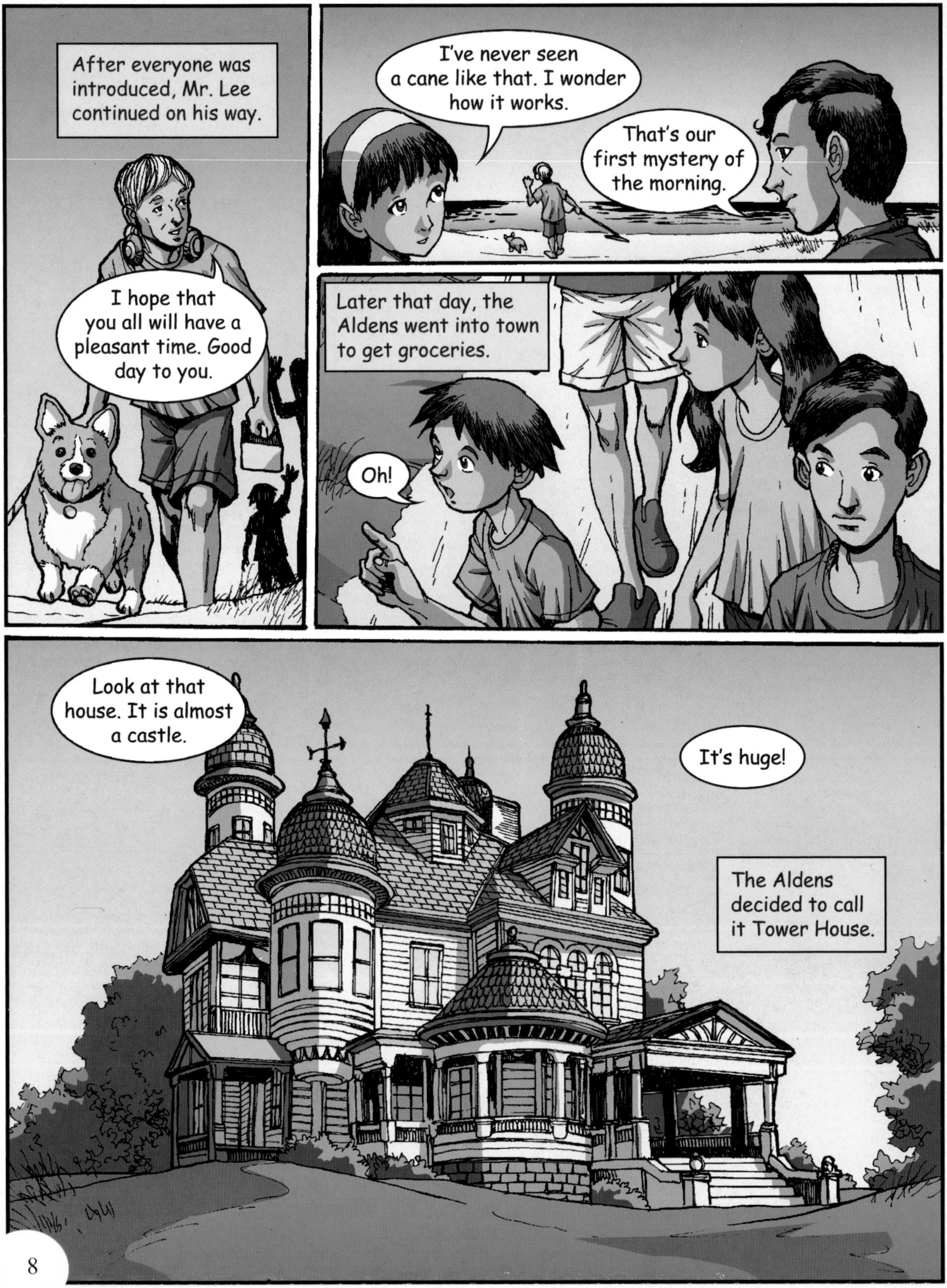
After everyone was introduced, Mr. Lee continued on his way.
I hope that you all will have a pleasant time. Good day to you.
I've never seen a cane like that. I wonder how it works.
That's our first mystery of the morning.
Later that day, the Aldens went into town to get groceries.
Oh!
Look at that house. It is almost a castle.
It's huge!
The Aldens decided to call it Tower House.

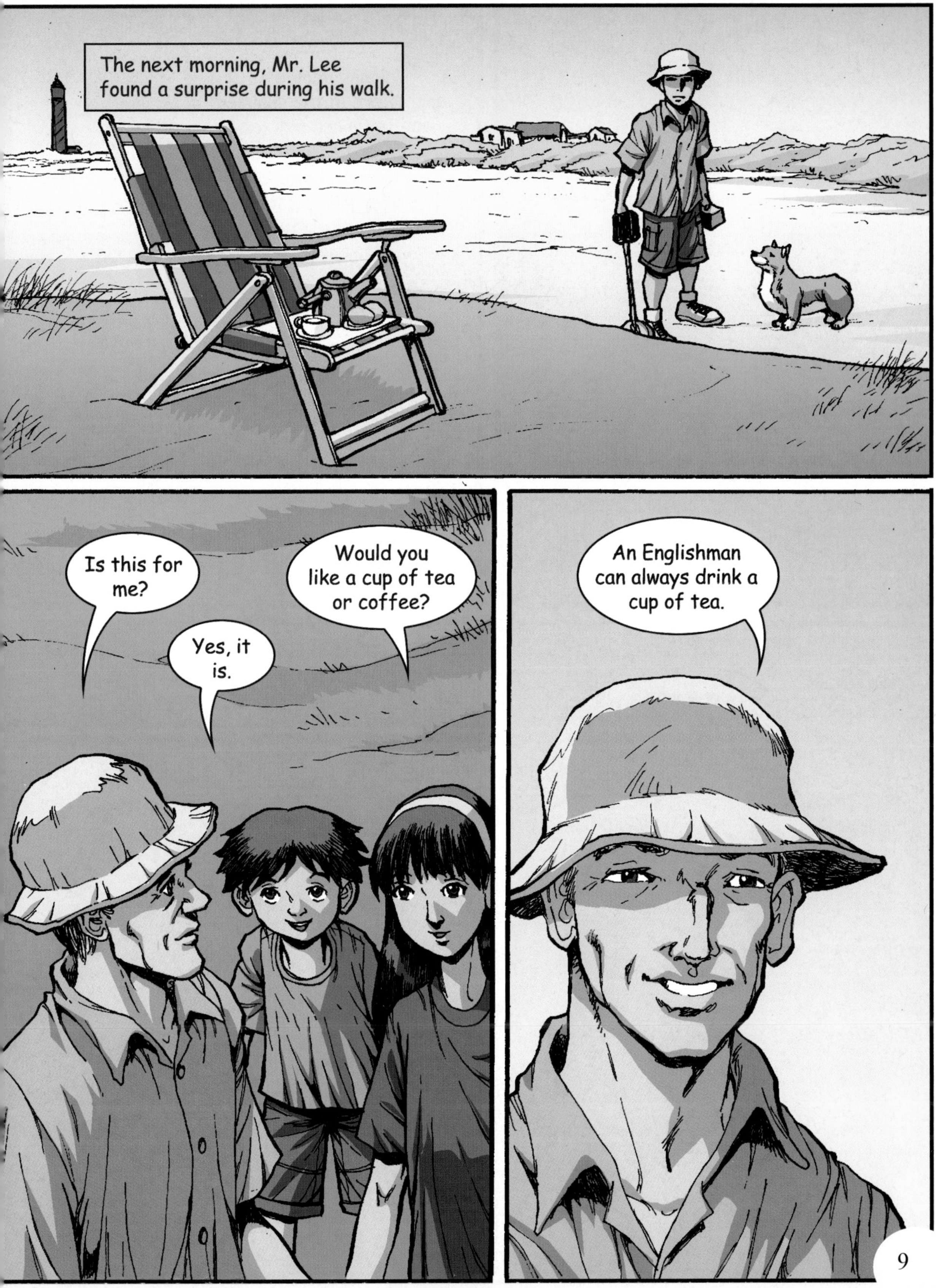
The next morning, Mr. Lee found a surprise during his walk.
Is this for me?
Yes, it is.
Would you like a cup of tea or coffee?
An Englishman can always drink a cup of tea.

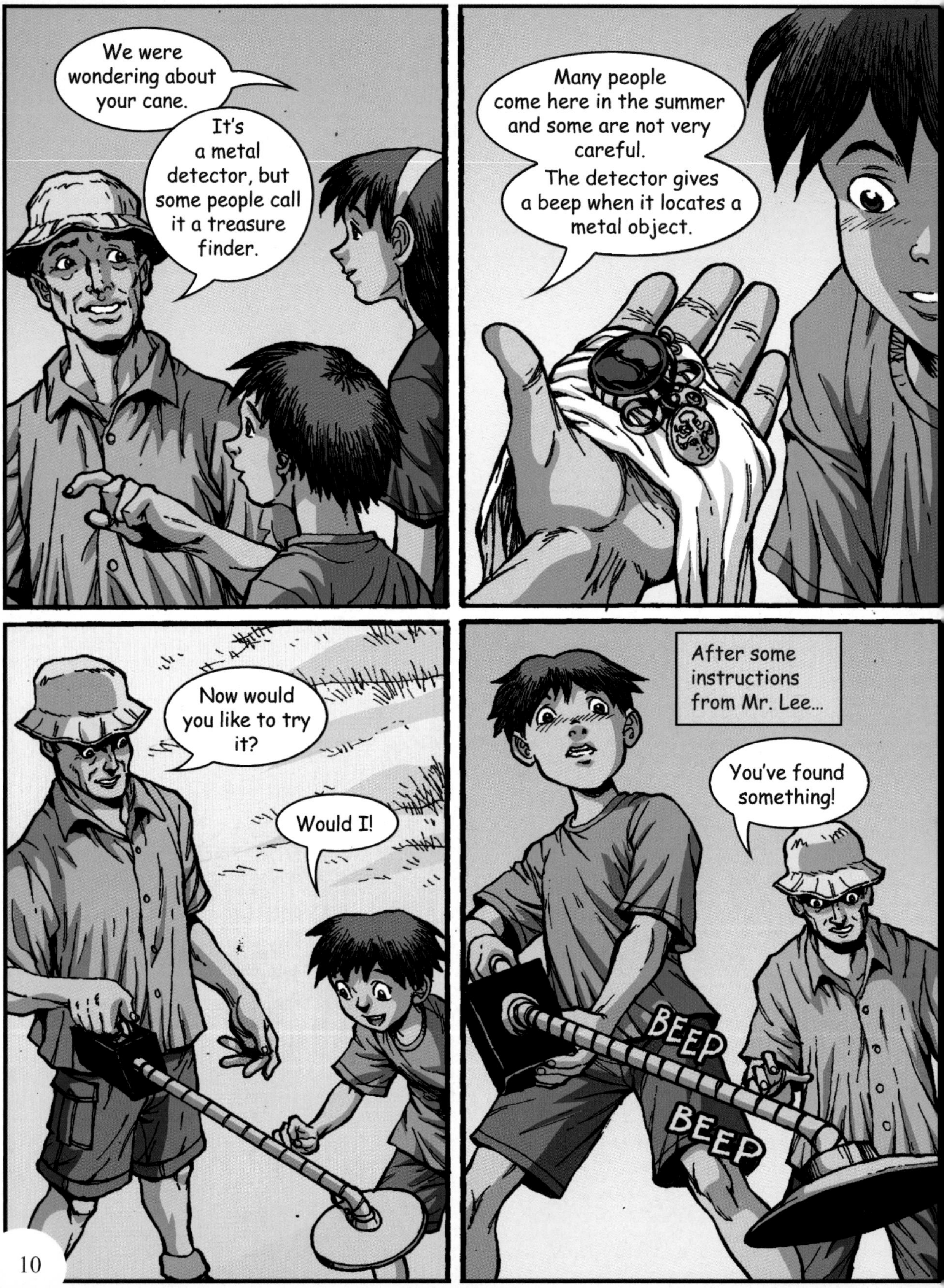
We were wondering about your cane.
It's a metal detector, but some people call it a treasure finder.
Many people come here in the summer and some are not very careful.
The detector gives a beep when it locates a metal object.
Now would you like to try it?
Would I!
After some instructions from Mr. Lee...
You've found something!
BEEP
BEEP

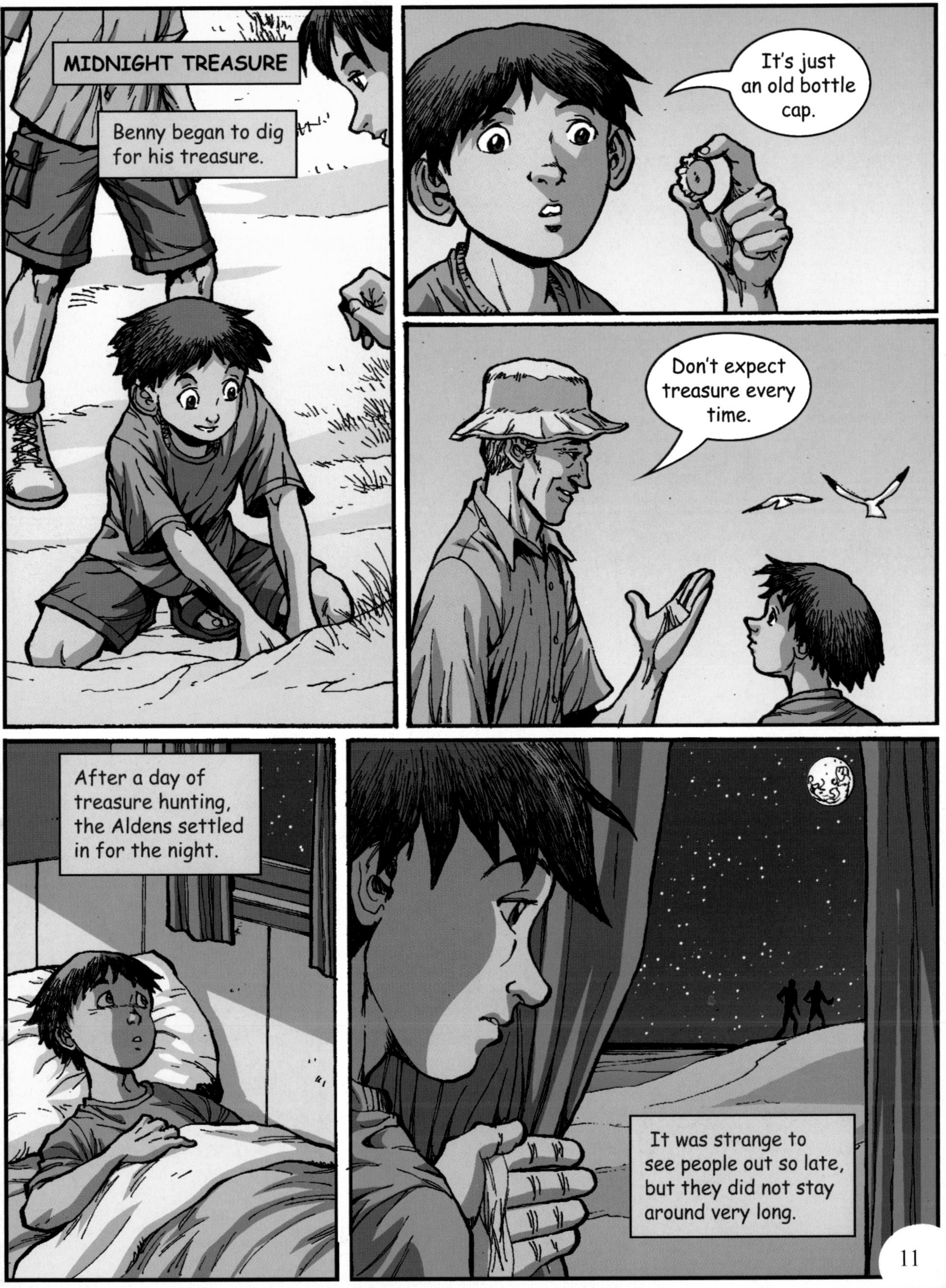
MIDNIGHT TREASURE
Benny began to dig for his treasure.
It's just an old bottle cap.
Don't expect treasure every time.
After a day of treasure hunting, the Aldens settled in for the night.
It was strange to see people out so late, but they did not stay around very long.

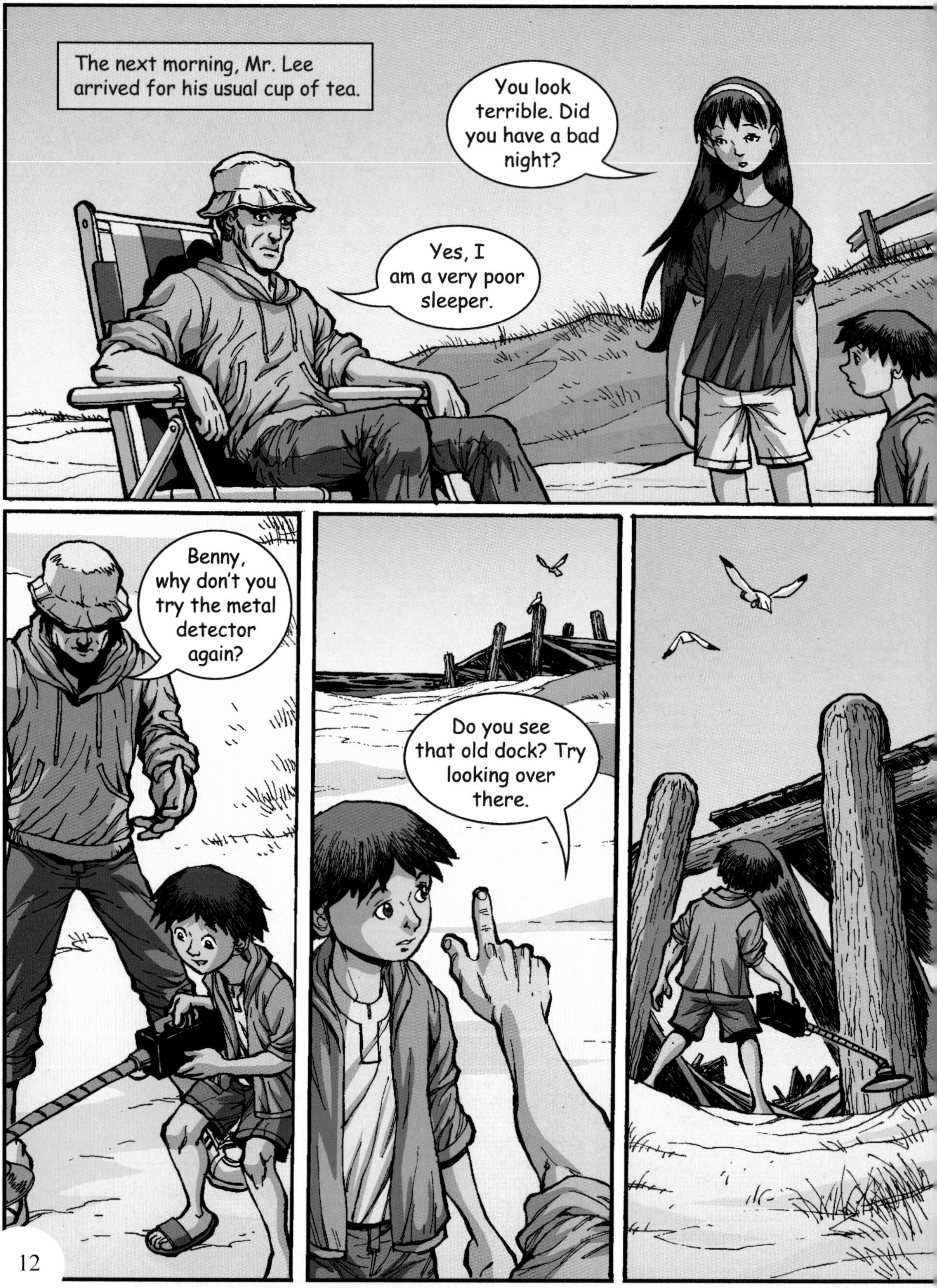
The next morning, Mr. Lee arrived for his usual cup of tea.
You look terrible. Did you have a bad night?
Yes, I am a very poor sleeper.
Benny, why don't you try the metal detector again?
Do you see that old dock? Try looking over there.

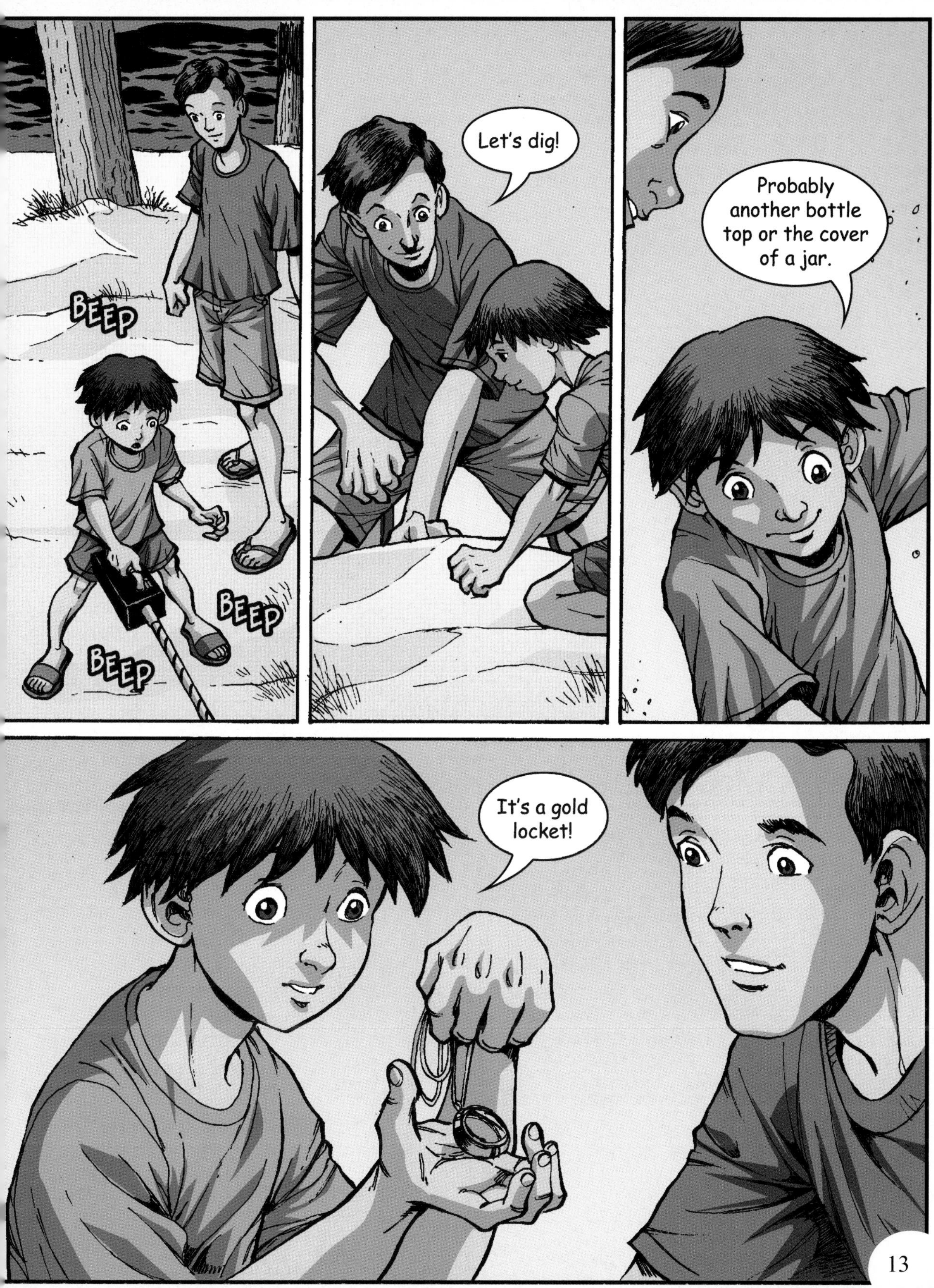
BEEP
BEEP
BEEP
Let's dig!
Probably another bottle top or the cover of a jar.
It's a gold locket!

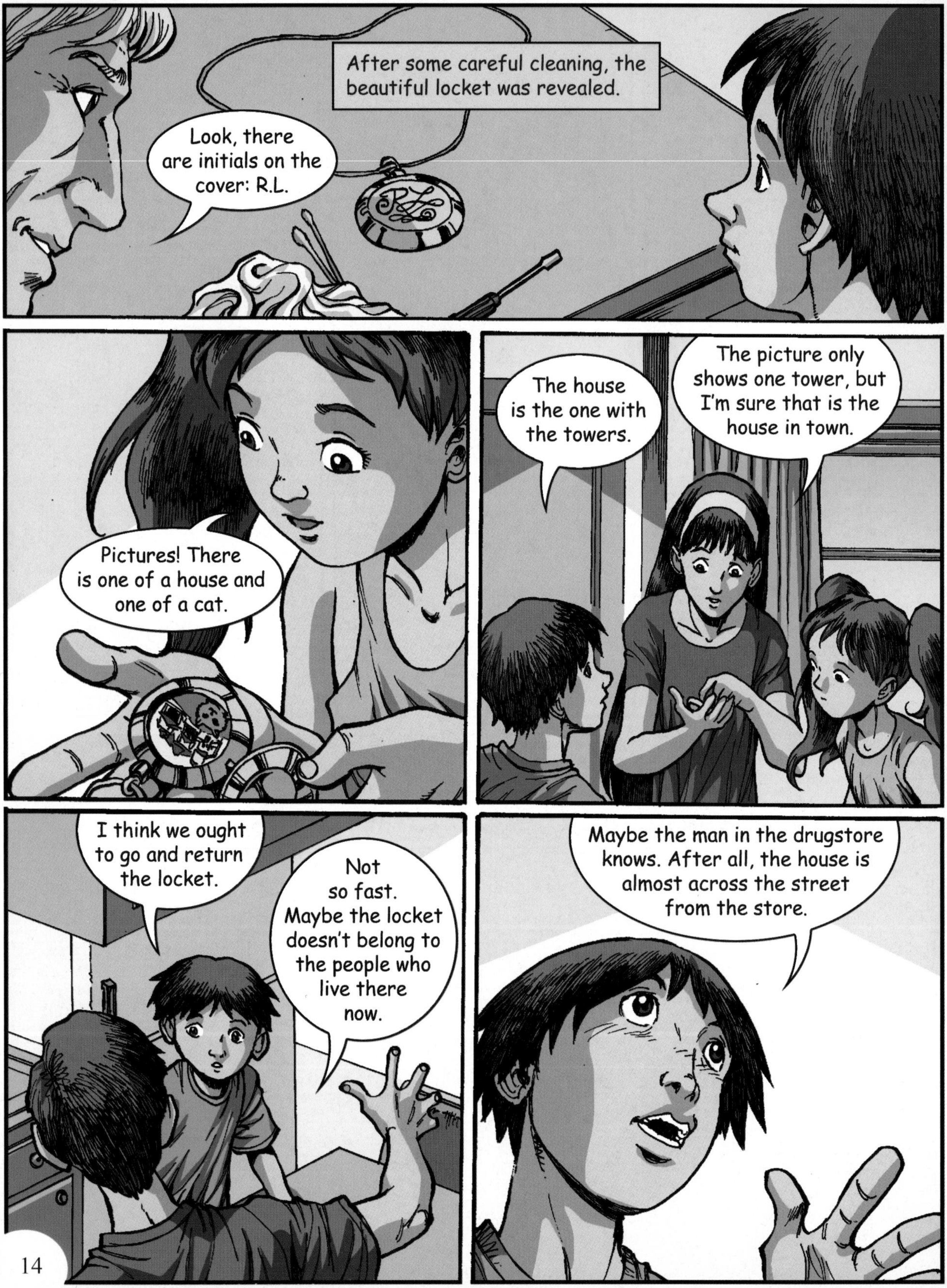

After some careful cleaning, the beautiful locket was revealed.
Look, there are initials on the cover: R.L.
Pictures! There is one of a house and one of a cat.
The house is the one with the towers.
The picture only shows one tower, but I'm sure that is the house in town.
I think we ought to go and return the locket.
Not so fast. Maybe the locket doesn't belong to the people who live there now.
Maybe the man in the drugstore knows. After all, the house is almost across the street from the store.

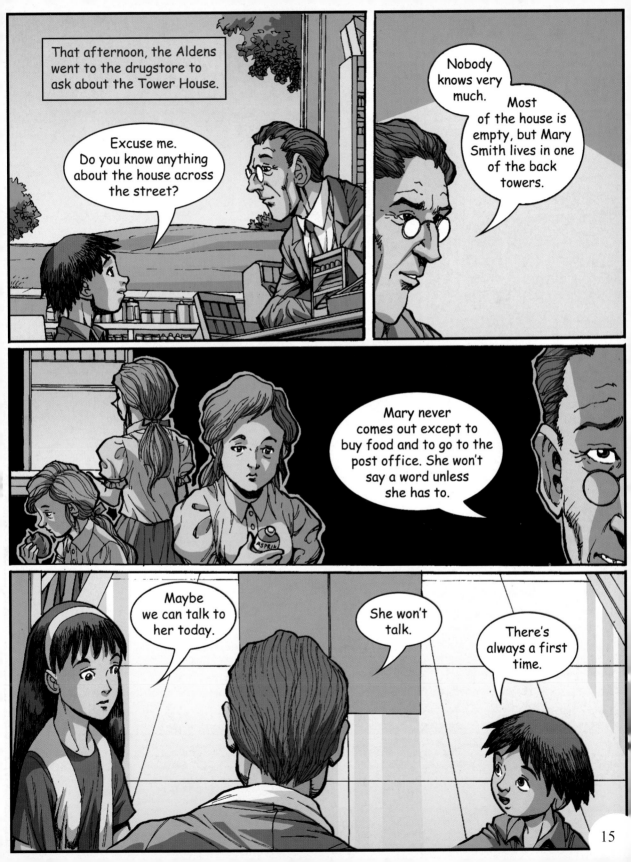

That afternoon, the Aldens went to the drugstore to ask about the Tower House.

Excuse me. Do you know anything about the house across the street?

Nobody knows very much. Most of the house is empty, but Mary Smith lives in one of the back towers.

Mary never comes out except to buy food and to go to the post office. She won't say a word unless she has to.

Maybe we can talk to her today.

She won't talk.

There's always a first time.

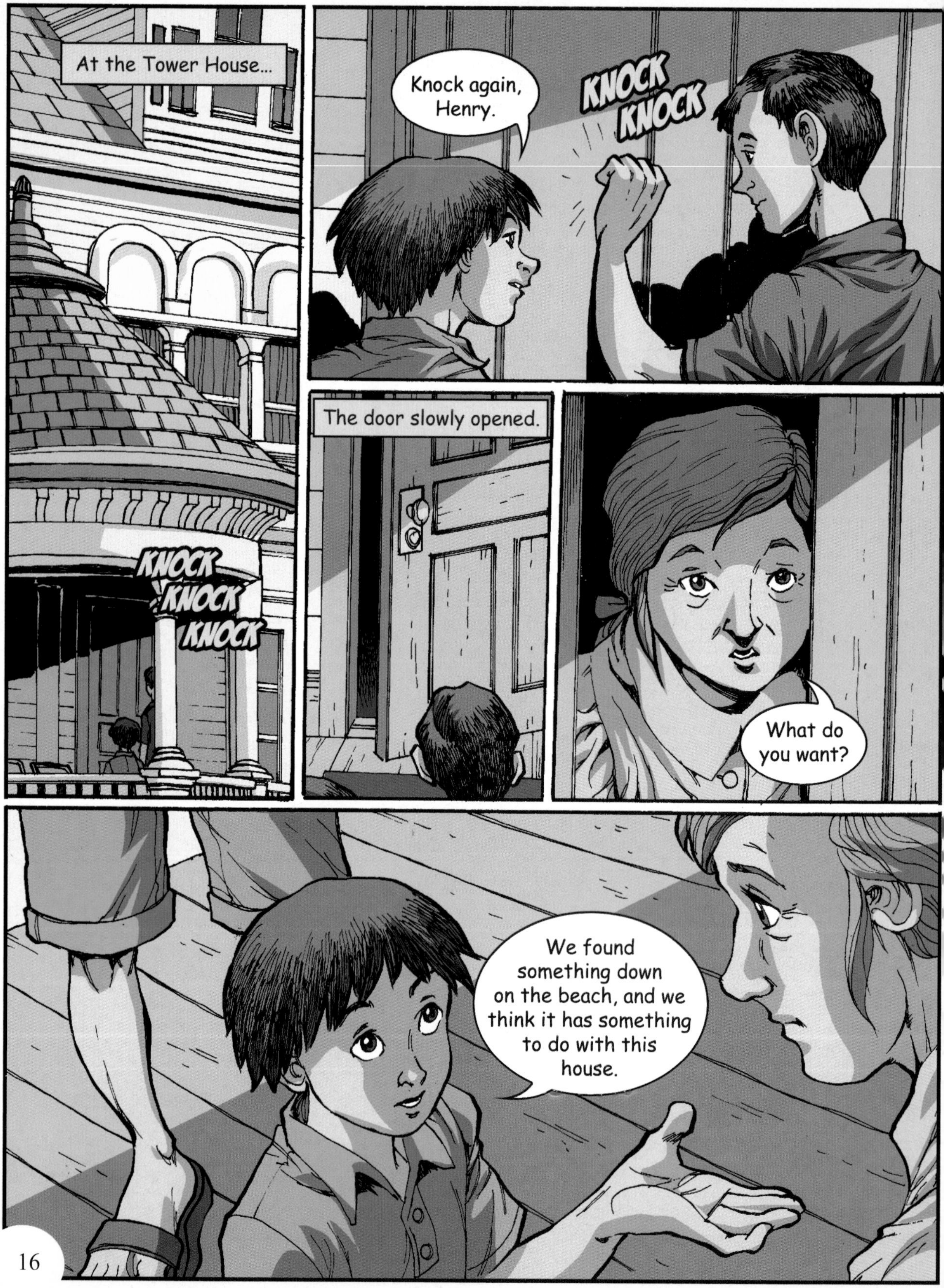
At the Tower House...
KNOCK
KNOCK
KNOCK
Knock again, Henry.
KNOCK
KNOCK
The door slowly opened.
What do you want?
We found something down on the beach, and we think it has something to do with this house.

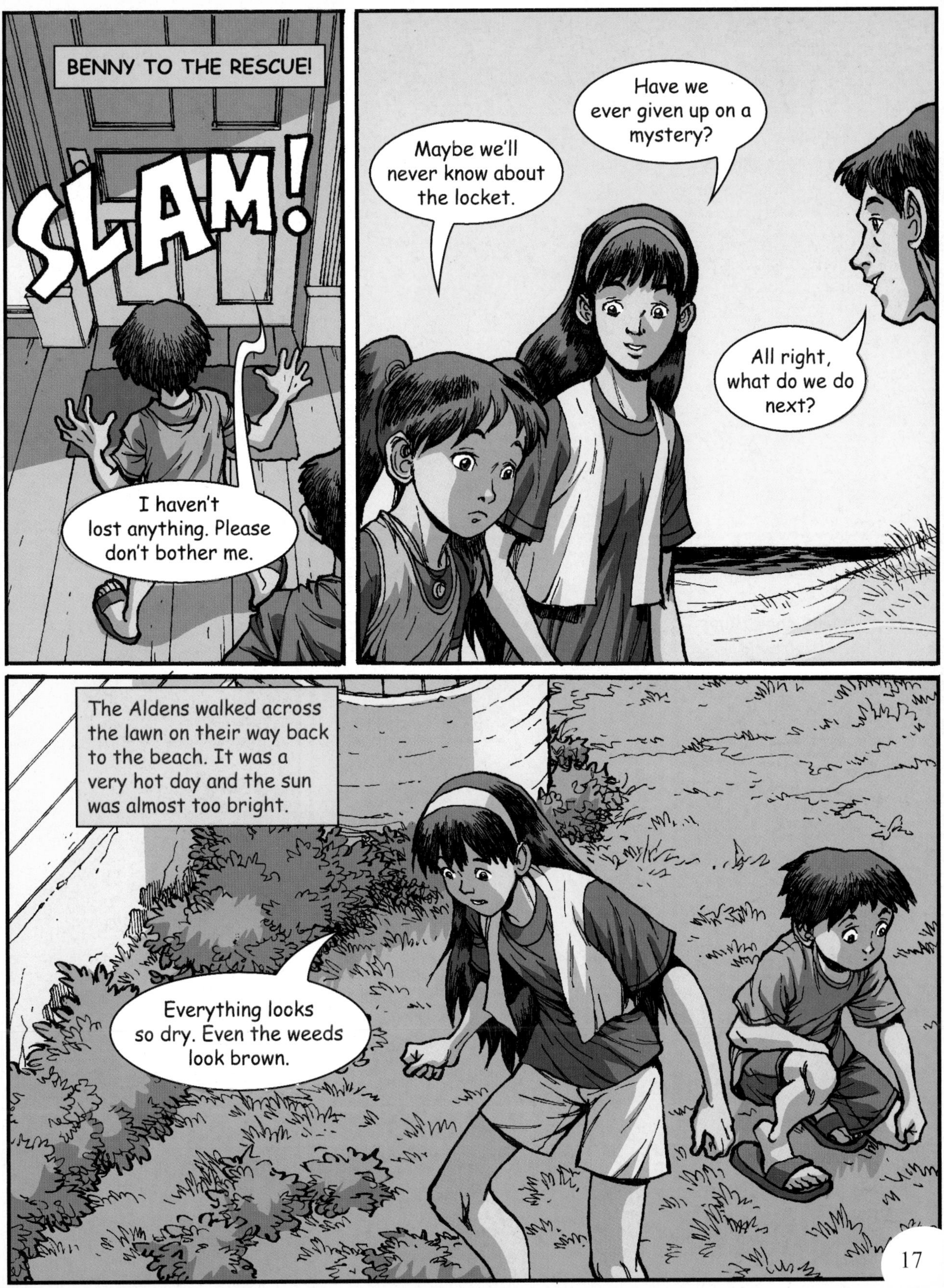
BENNY TO THE RESCUE!
SLAM!
I haven't lost anything. Please don't bother me.
Maybe we'll never know about the locket.
Have we ever given up on a mystery?
All right, what do we do next?
The Aldens walked across the lawn on their way back to the beach. It was a very hot day and the sun was almost too bright.
Everything looks so dry. Even the weeds look brown.

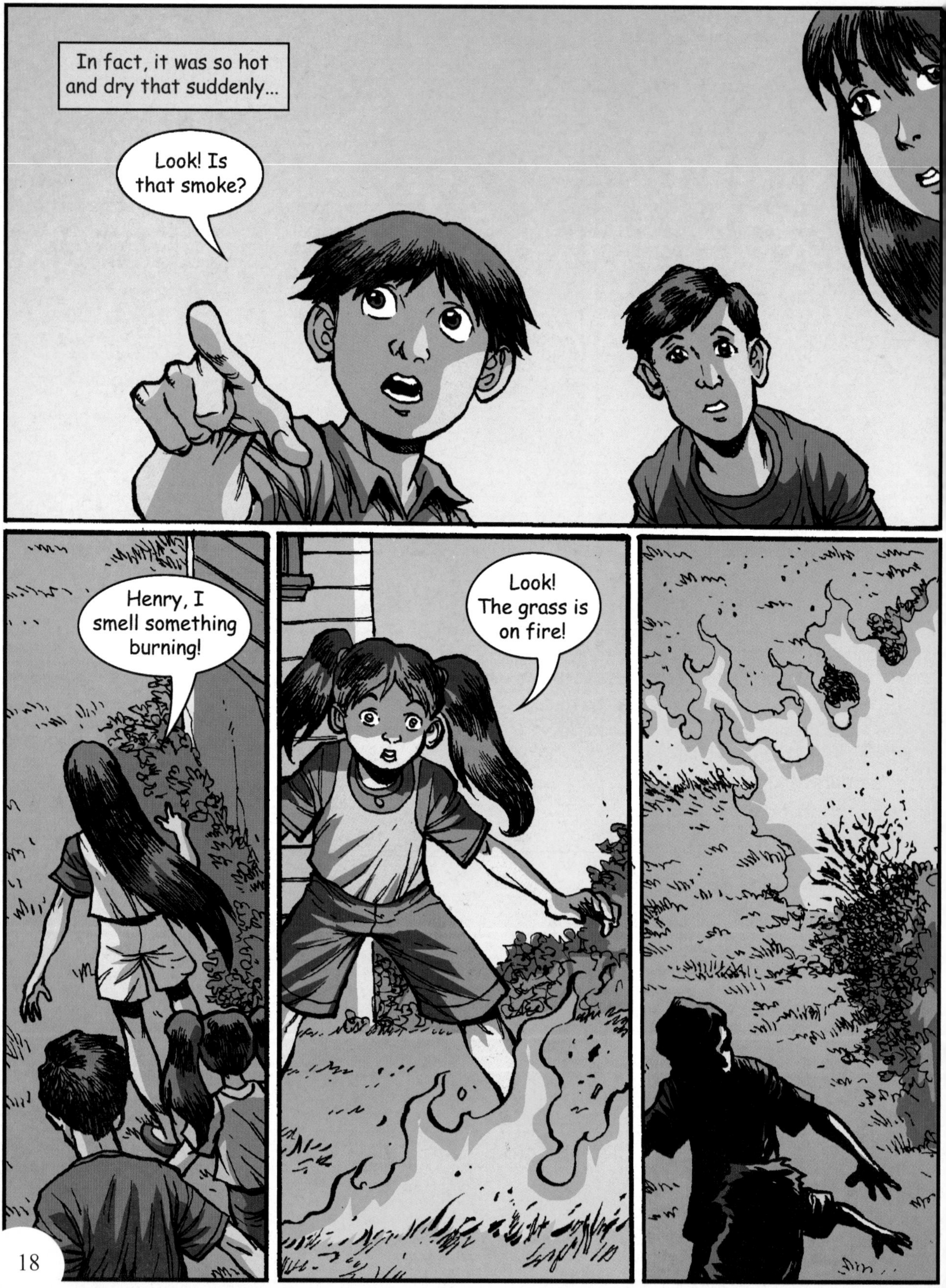
In fact, it was so hot and dry that suddenly...
Look! Is that smoke?
Henry, I smell something burning!
Look! The grass is on fire!

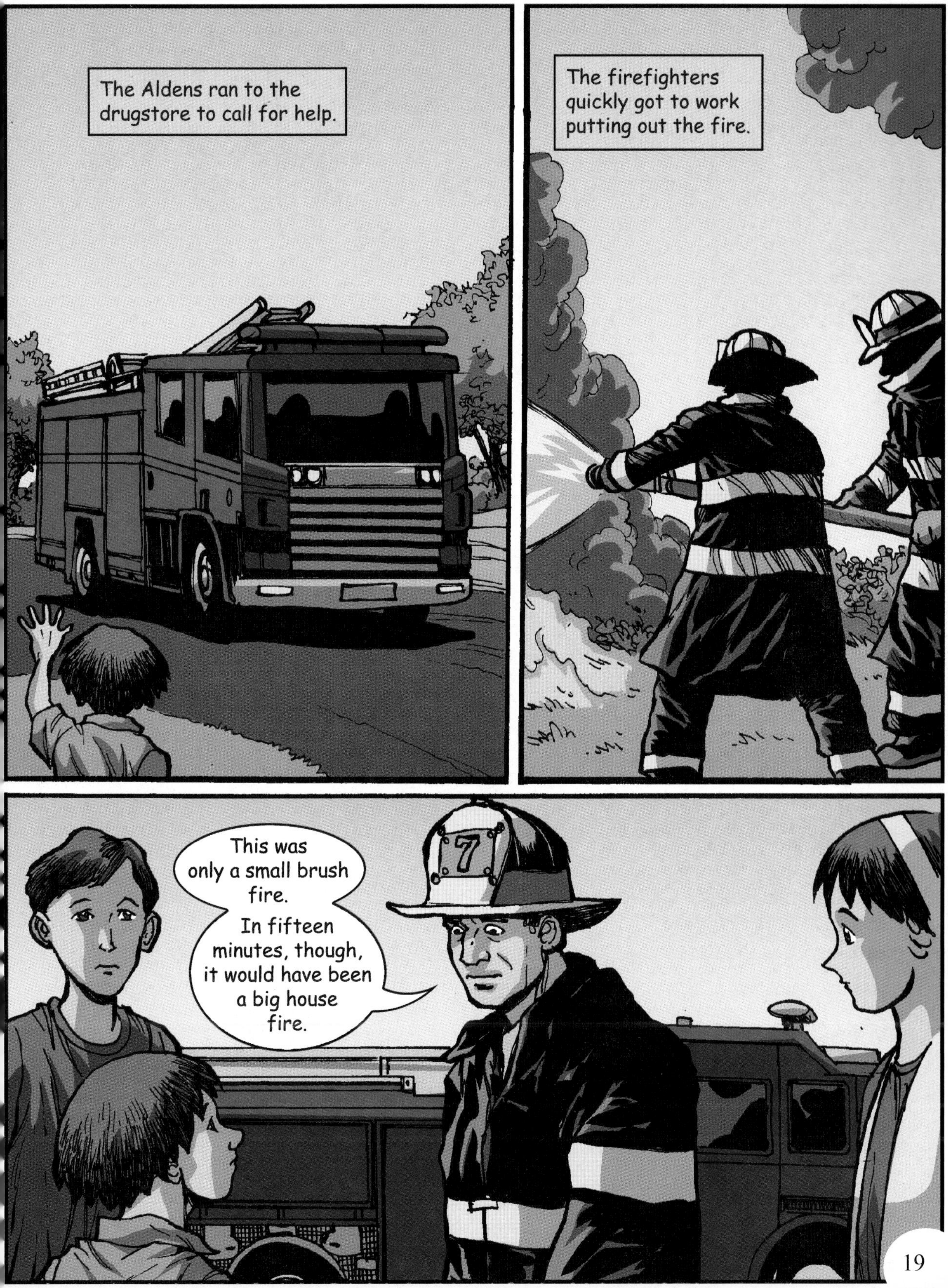

The Aldens ran to the drugstore to call for help.
The firefighters quickly got to work putting out the fire.
This was only a small brush fire.
In fifteen minutes, though, it would have been a big house fire.
7

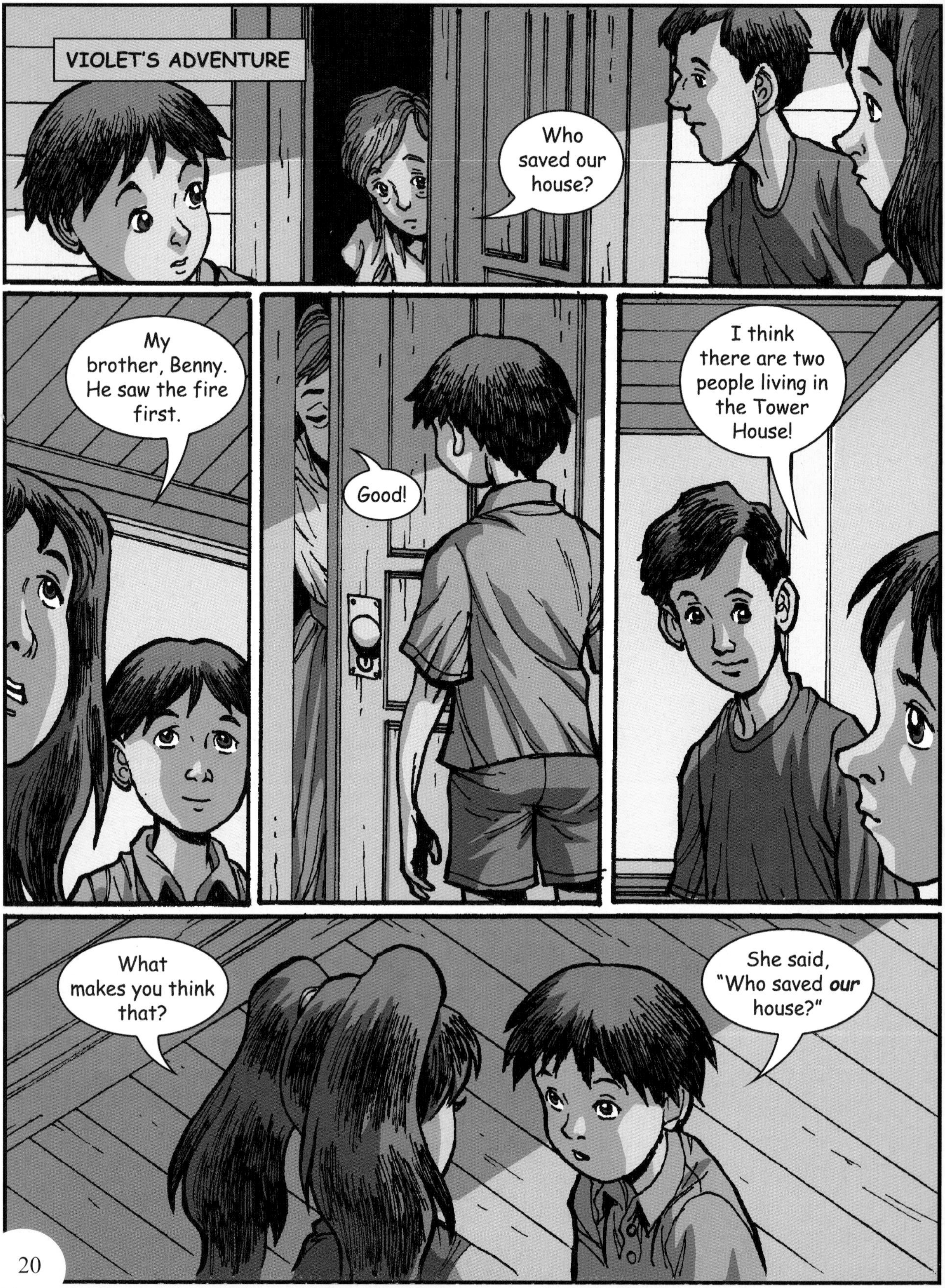
VIOLET'S ADVENTURE
Who saved our house?
My brother, Benny. He saw the fire first.
Good!
I think there are two people living in the Tower House!
What makes you think that?
She said, "Who saved **our** house?"

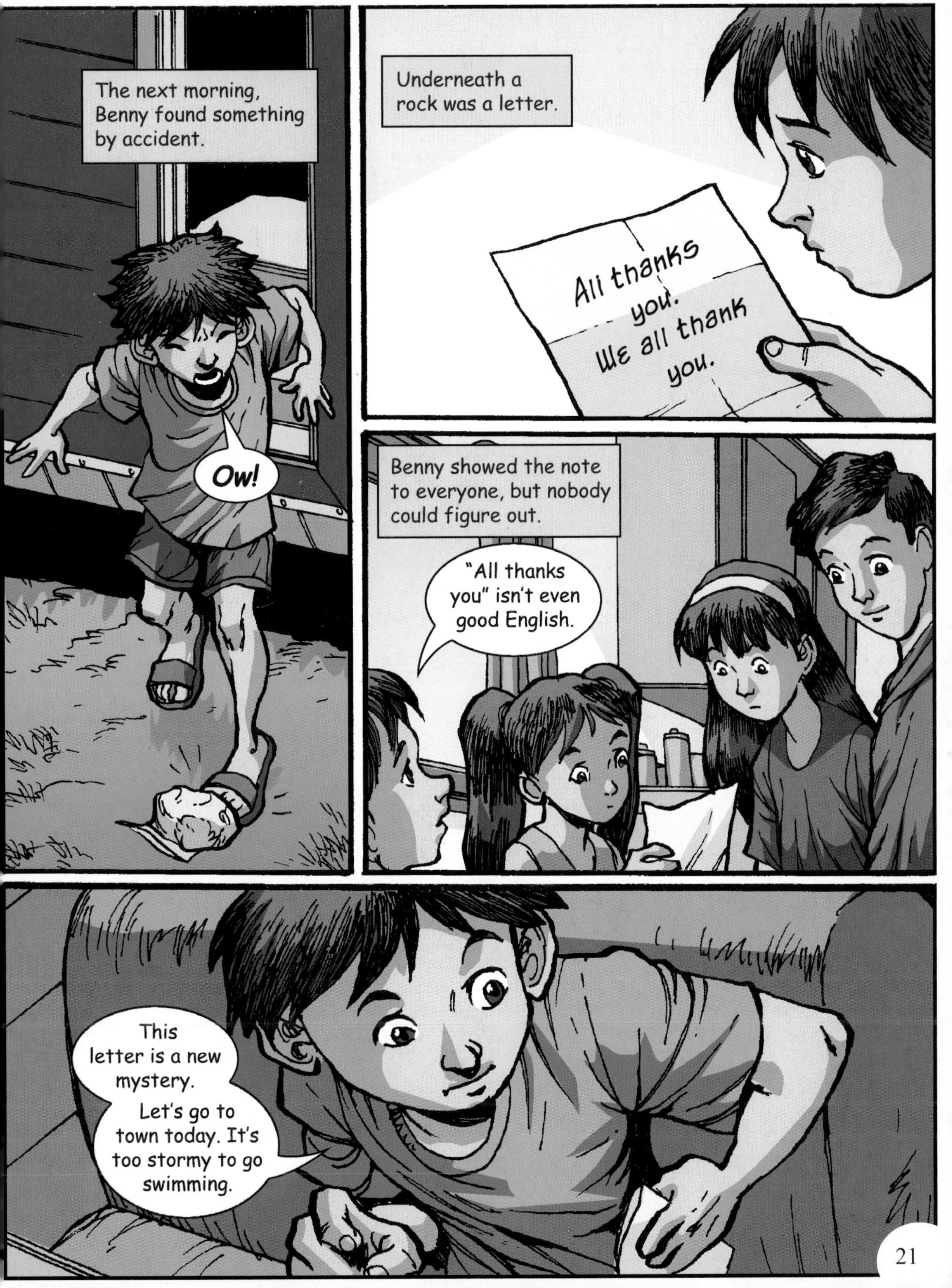

The next morning, Benny found something by accident.
Ow!
Underneath a rock was a letter.
All thanks you. We all thank you.
Benny showed the note to everyone, but nobody could figure out.
"All thanks you" isn't even good English.
This letter is a new mystery.
Let's go to town today. It's too stormy to go swimming.

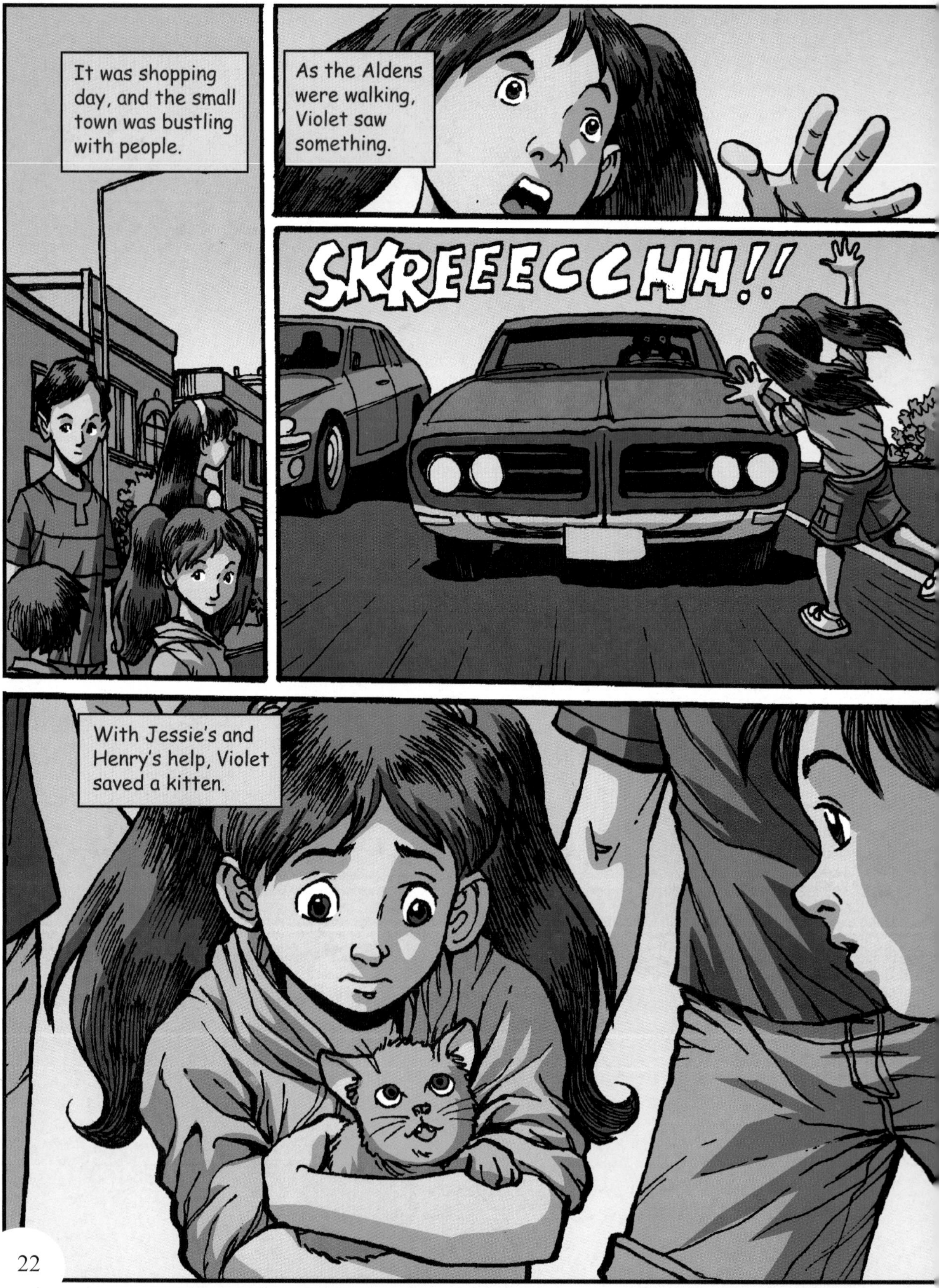
It was shopping day, and the small town was bustling with people.
As the Aldens were walking, Violet saw something.
SKREEECCHH!!
With Jessie's and Henry's help, Violet saved a kitten.

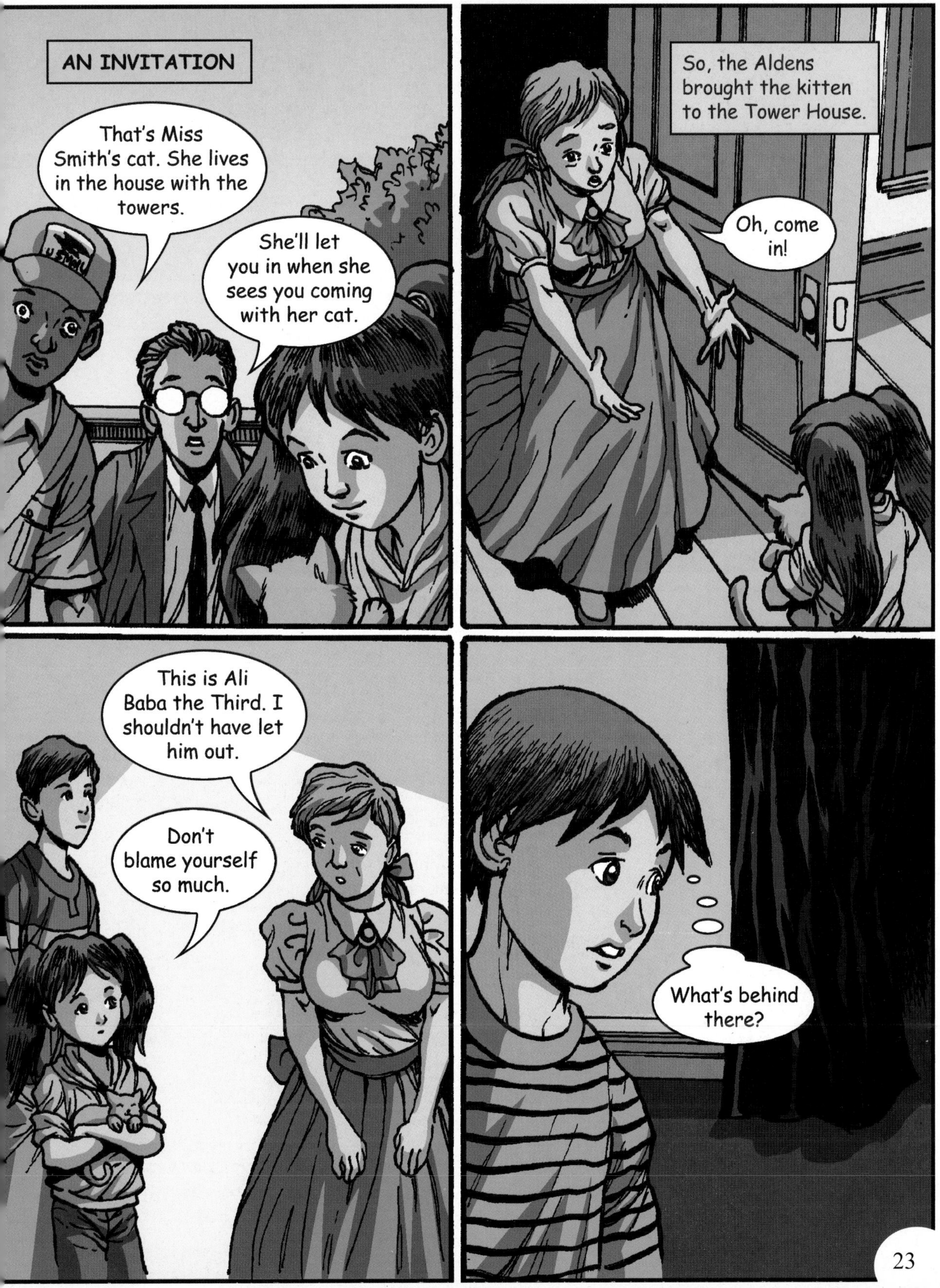
AN INVITATION
That's Miss Smith's cat. She lives in the house with the towers.
She'll let you in when she sees you coming with her cat.
So, the Aldens brought the kitten to the Tower House.
Oh, come in!
This is Ali Baba the Third. I shouldn't have let him out.
Don't blame yourself so much.
What's behind there?

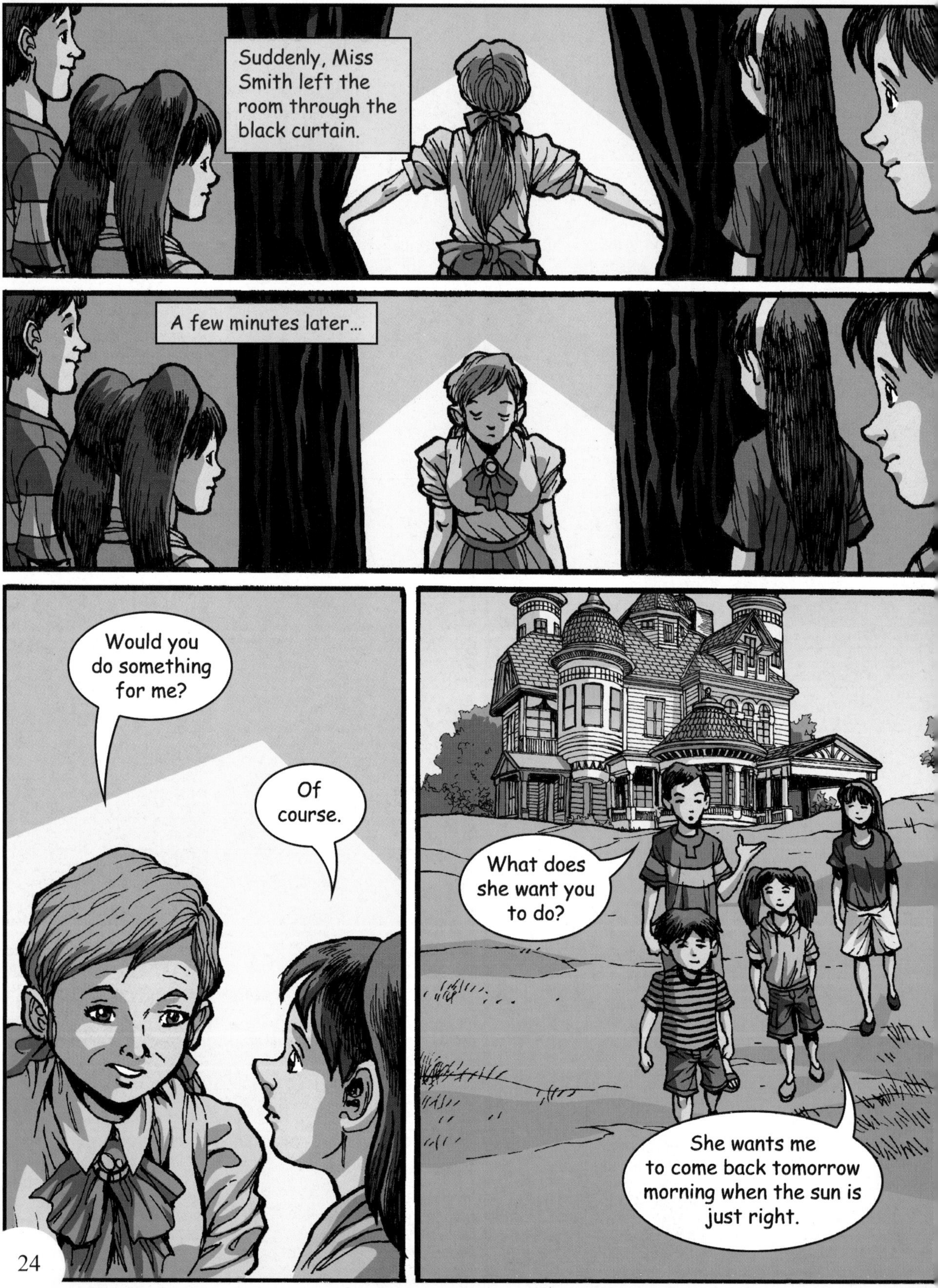
Suddenly, Miss Smith left the room through the black curtain.
A few minutes later...
Would you do something for me?
Of course.
What does she want you to do?
She wants me to come back tomorrow morning when the sun is just right.

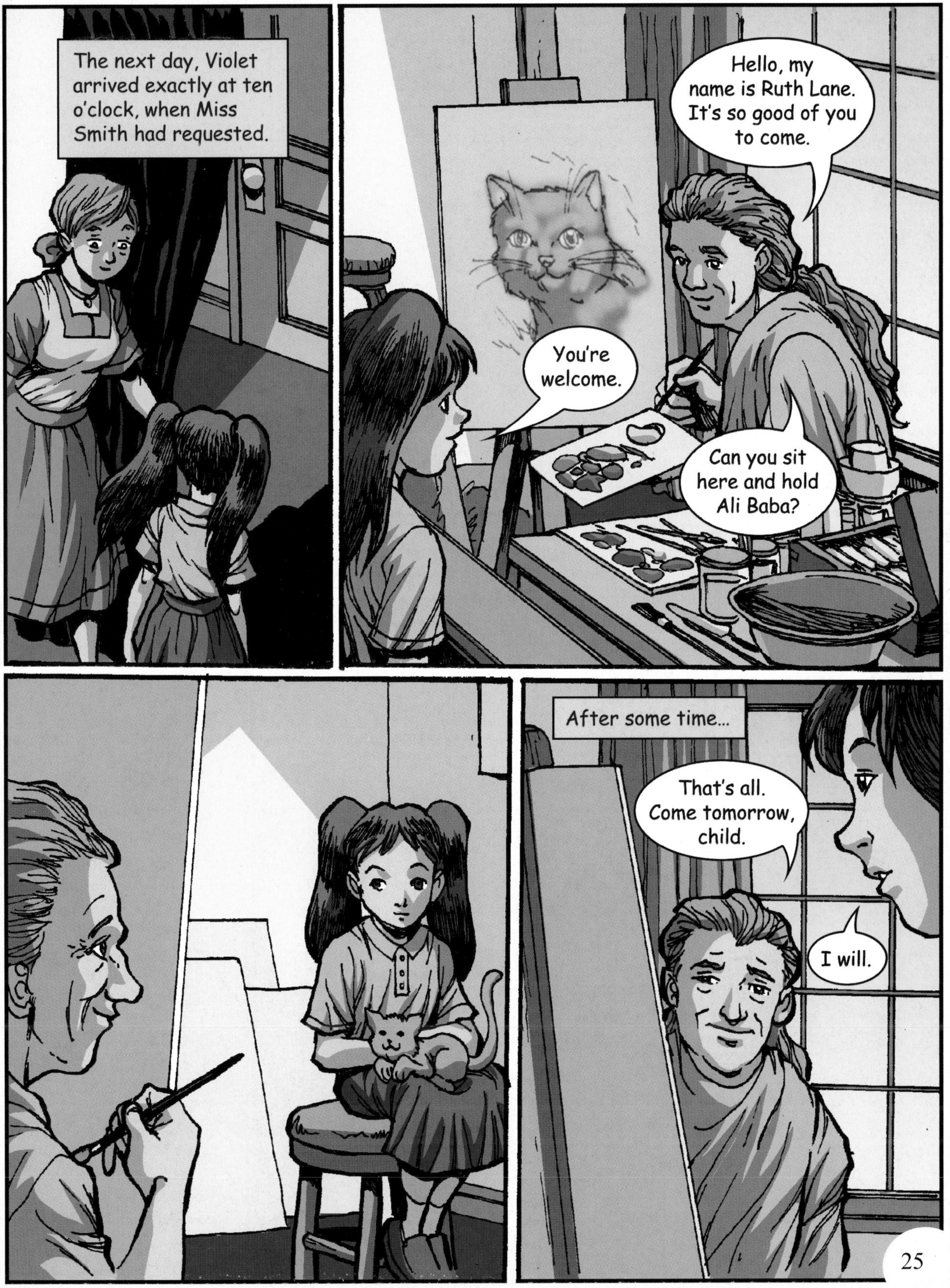
The next day, Violet arrived exactly at ten o'clock, when Miss Smith had requested.
Hello, my name is Ruth Lane. It's so good of you to come.
You're welcome.
Can you sit here and hold Ali Baba?
After some time...
That's all. Come tomorrow, child.
I will.

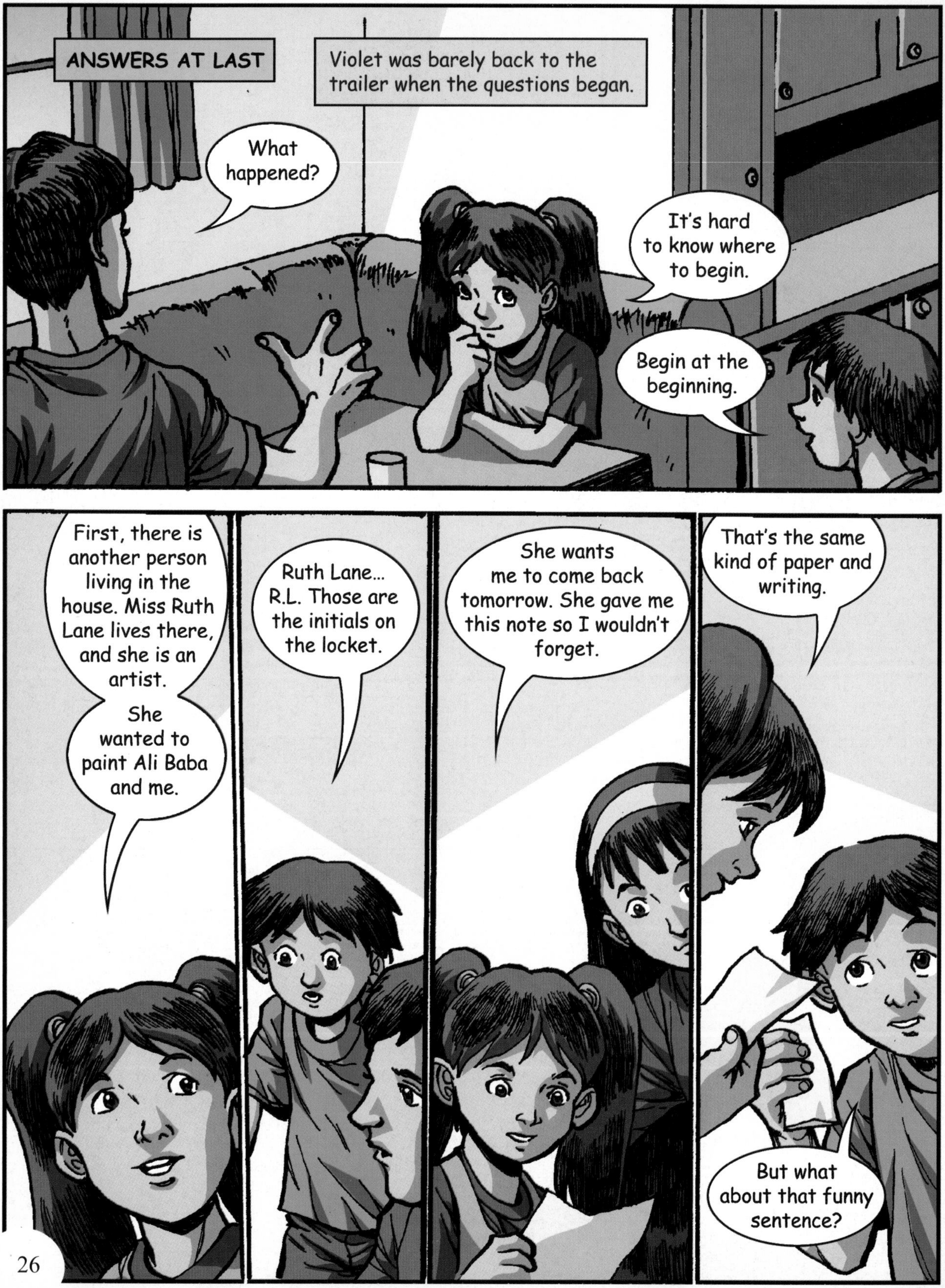
ANSWERS AT LAST
Violet was barely back to the trailer when the questions began.
What happened?
It's hard to know where to begin.
Begin at the beginning.
First, there is another person living in the house. Miss Ruth Lane lives there, and she is an artist.
She wanted to paint Ali Baba and me.
Ruth Lane... R.L. Those are the initials on the locket.
She wants me to come back tomorrow. She gave me this note so I wouldn't forget.
That's the same kind of paper and writing.
But what about that funny sentence?

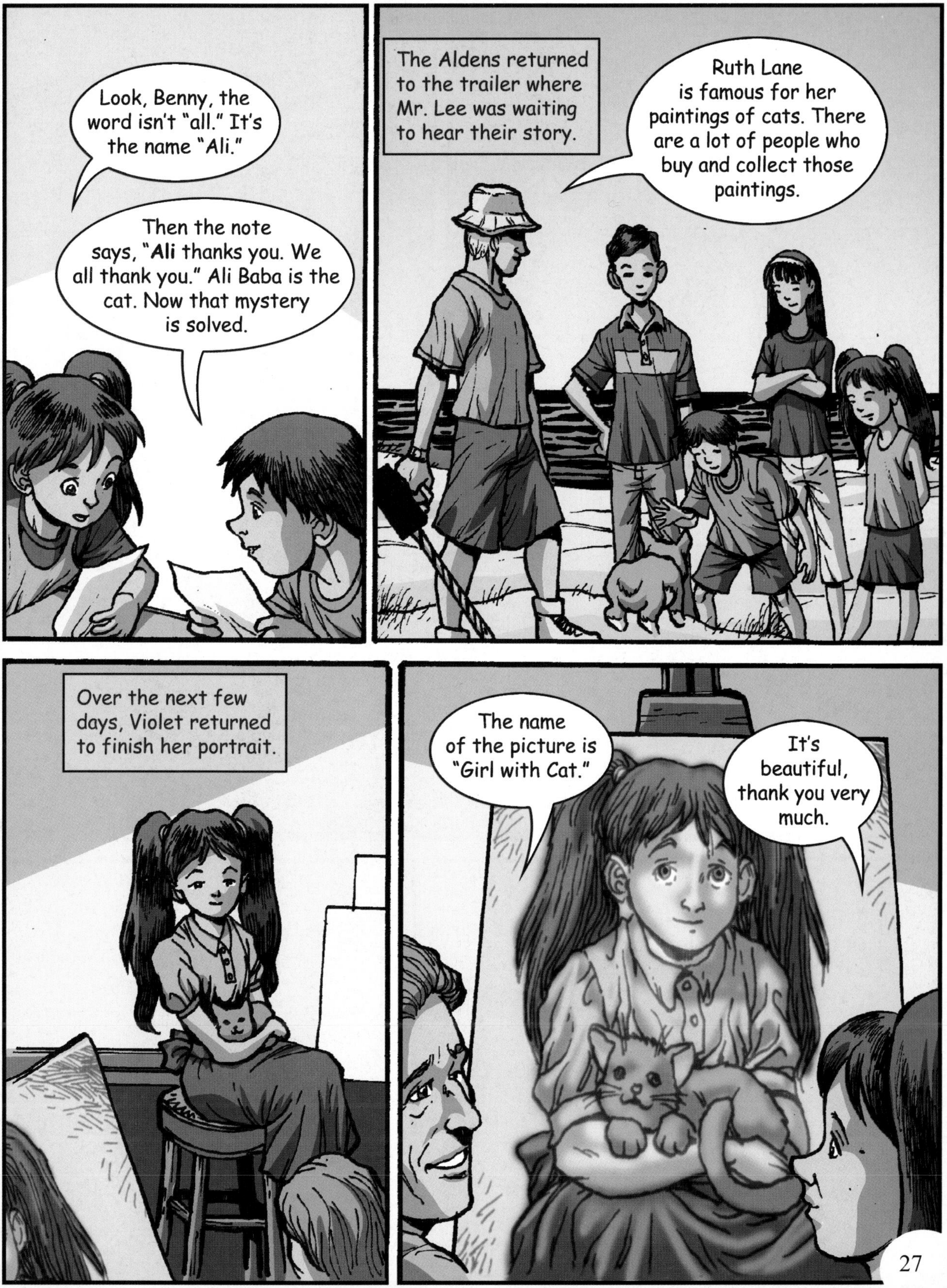

Look, Benny, the word isn't "all." It's the name "Ali."
Then the note says, "**Ali** thanks you. We all thank you." Ali Baba is the cat. Now that mystery is solved.
The Aldens returned to the trailer where Mr. Lee was waiting to hear their story.
Ruth Lane is famous for her paintings of cats. There are a lot of people who buy and collect those paintings.
Over the next few days, Violet returned to finish her portrait.
The name of the picture is "Girl with Cat."
It's beautiful, thank you very much.

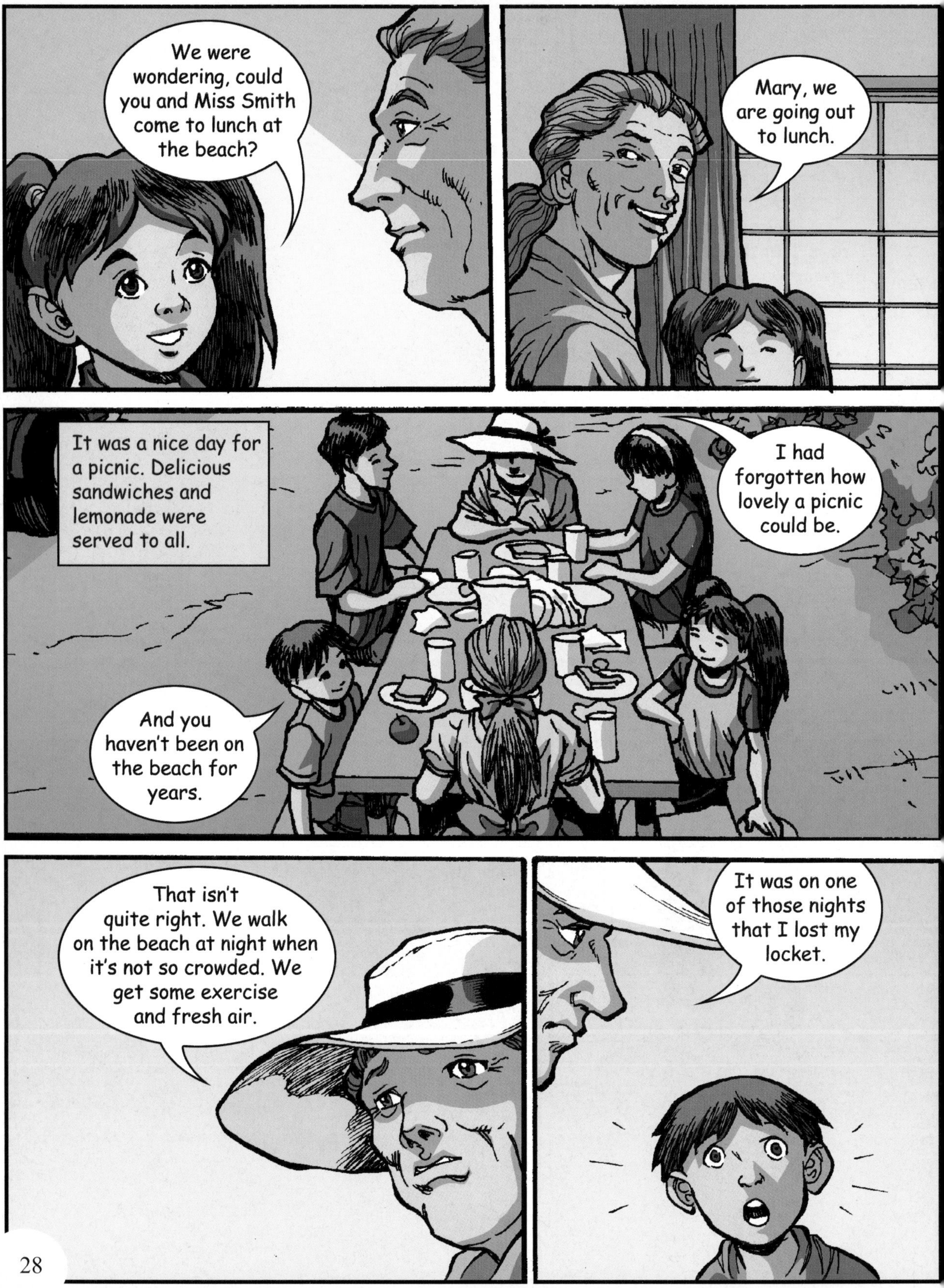
We were wondering, could you and Miss Smith come to lunch at the beach?
Mary, we are going out to lunch.
It was a nice day for a picnic. Delicious sandwiches and lemonade were served to all.
I had forgotten how lovely a picnic could be.
And you haven't been on the beach for years.
That isn't quite right. We walk on the beach at night when it's not so crowded. We get some exercise and fresh air.
It was on one of those nights that I lost my locket.

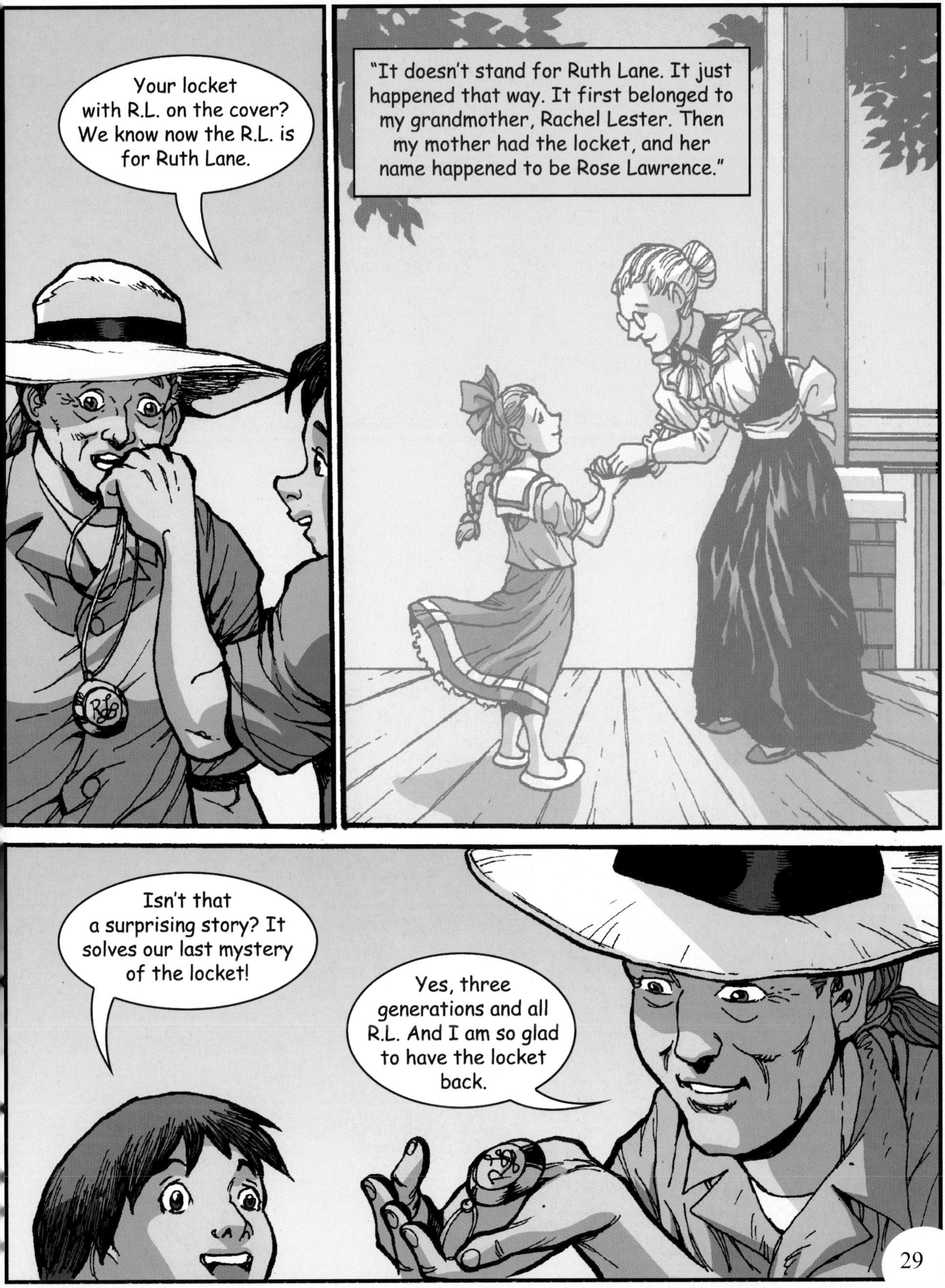
Your locket with R.L. on the cover? We know now the R.L. is for Ruth Lane.
"It doesn't stand for Ruth Lane. It just happened that way. It first belonged to my grandmother, Rachel Lester. Then my mother had the locket, and her name happened to be Rose Lawrence."
Isn't that a surprising story? It solves our last mystery of the locket!
Yes, three generations and all R.L. And I am so glad to have the locket back.

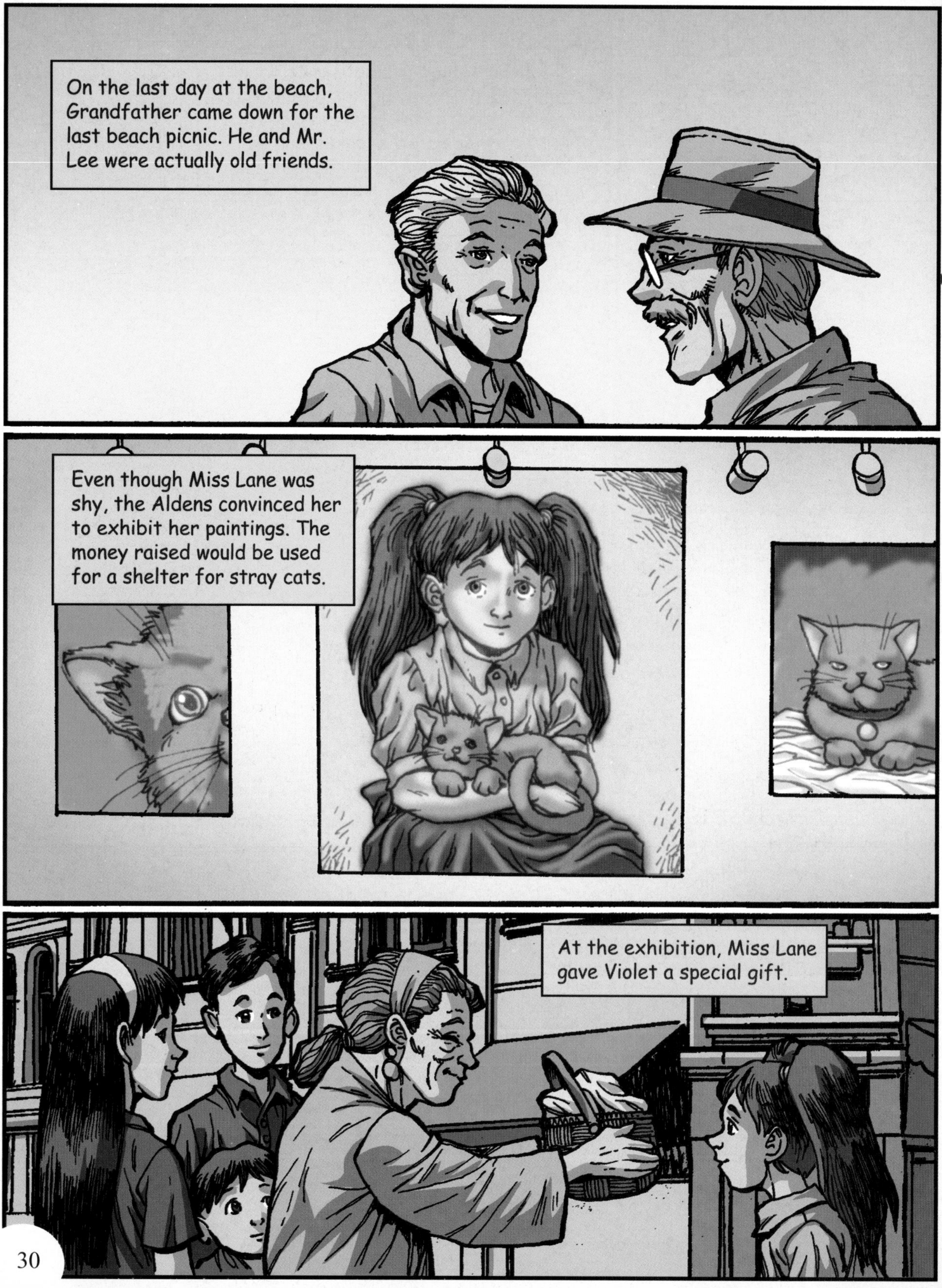
On the last day at the beach, Grandfather came down for the last beach picnic. He and Mr. Lee were actually old friends.
Even though Miss Lane was shy, the Aldens convinced her to exhibit her paintings. The money raised would be used for a shelter for stray cats.
At the exhibition, Miss Lane gave Violet a special gift.

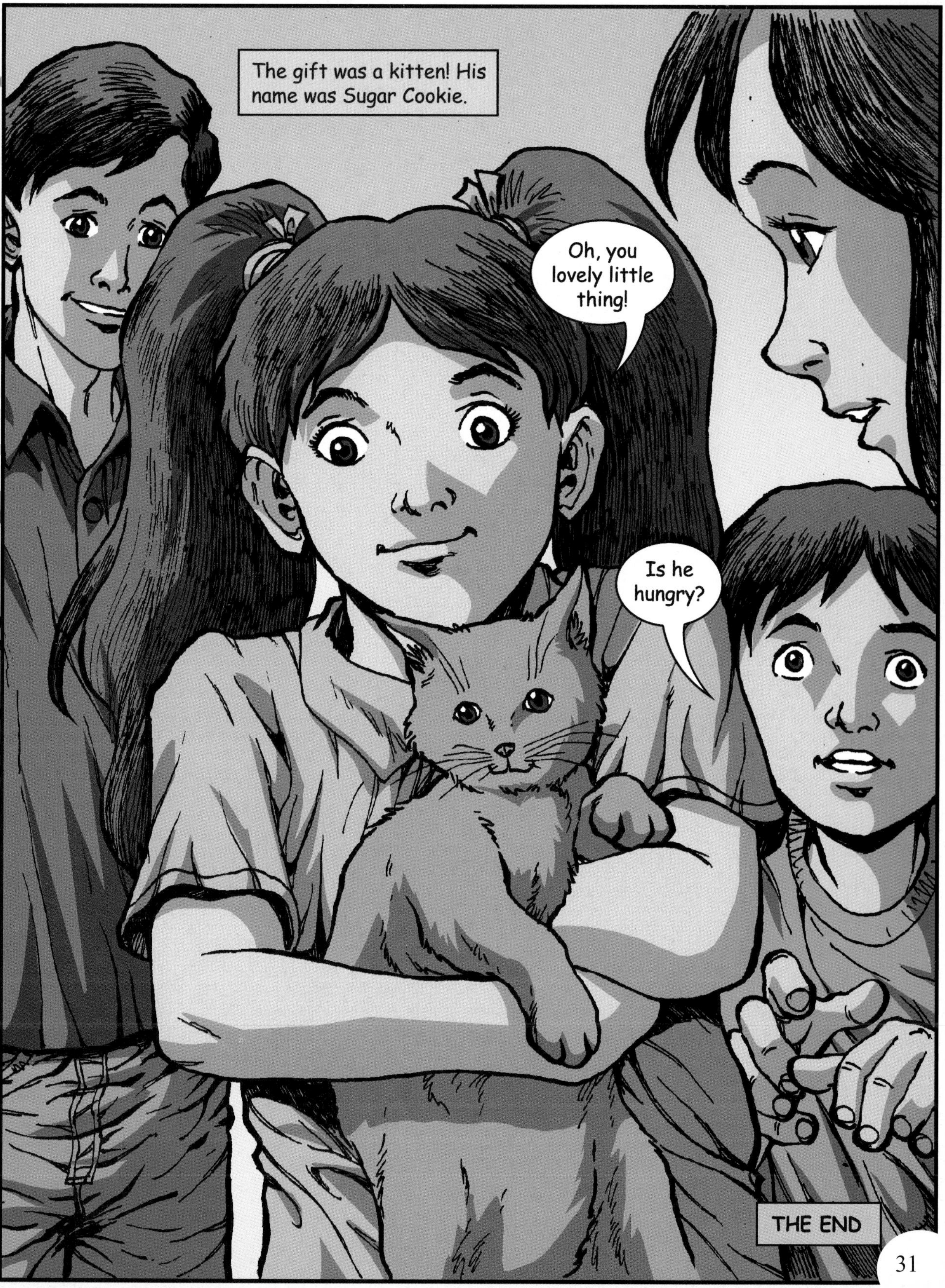
The gift was a kitten! His name was Sugar Cookie.
Oh, you lovely little thing!
Is he hungry?
THE END

ABOUT THE CREATOR

Gertrude Chandler Warner was born on April 16, 1890, in Putnam, Connecticut. In 1918, Warner began teaching at Israel Putnam School. As a teacher, she discovered that many readers who liked an exciting story could not find books that were both easy and fun to read. She decided to try to meet this need. In 1942, *The Boxcar Children* was published for these readers.

Warner drew on her own experience to write *The Boxcar Children.* As a child she spent hours watching trains go by on the tracks near her family home. She often dreamed about what it would be like to live in a caboose or freight car—just as the Alden children do.

When readers asked for more Alden adventures, Warner began additional stories. While the mystery element is central to each of the books, she never thought of them as strictly juvenile mysteries. She liked to stress the Aldens' independence. Henry, Jessie, Violet, and Benny go about most of their adventures with as little adult supervision as possible—something that delights young readers.

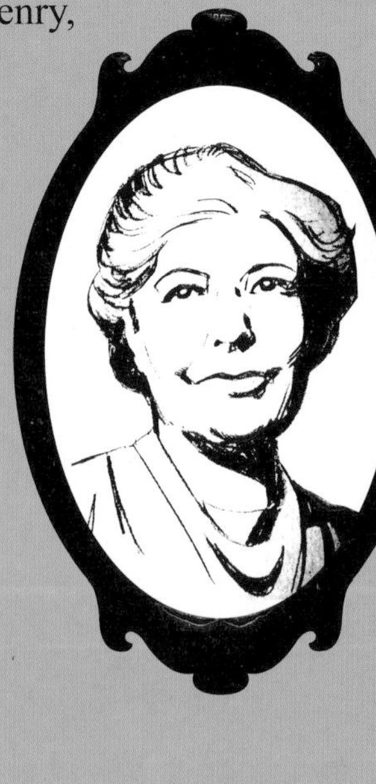

During her lifetime, Warner received hundreds of letters from fans as she continued the Aldens' adventures, writing nineteen Boxcar Children books in all. After her death in 1979, her publisher, Albert Whitman and Company, carried on Warner's vision. Today, the Boxcar Children series has more than 100 books.